TWIT

The owl who wasn't wise

There are lots of Early Reader stories you might enjoy.

Look at the back of the book or, for a complete list, visit www.orionbooks.co.uk

TWIT

The owl who wasn't wise

By Steve Cole

Illustrated by Jane Porter

Orion
Children's Books

First published in Great Britain in 2013
by Orion Children's Books
a division of the Orion Publishing Group Ltd
Orion House
5 Upper Saint Martin's Lane
London WC2H 9EA
An Hachette UK Company

1 3 5 7 9 10 8 6 4 2

The Orion Publishing Group's policy is to use papers that are
natural, renewable and recyclable products and made from wood
grown in sustainable forests. The logging and manufacturing
processes are expected to conform to the environmental
regulations of the country of origin.

A catalogue record for this book
is available from the British Library.

Printed and bound in China

www.orionbooks.co.uk

For Amy, always

Contents

Chapter One   11

Chapter Two   23

Chapter Three   31

Chapter Four   41

Chapter Five   57

Chapter One

Owls are wise. That's what people say.

Owls have big, wide eyes, so
they are always watching.

Owls stay up all night so they have lots of time to learn new things.

Owls see in the dark so they are clever at spotting things.

But there was once a little
owl who was different.

He lived with his brothers
in a tree in the middle of
a forest. This little owl was
called Twit.

Twit had orange eyes, wonky wings and scruffy feathers.

He was very nice, and very kind. But he wasn't very wise at all.

"Twit's a Twit!" hooted
Twit's mean brothers –
Boggle, Bumf and Baffle.

Every evening, the little owl would jump up from his bed with questions bursting out of his beak.

"What?"

"Where?"

"When?"

"Who?"

"Twit ter-wooo?"

"Button your beak!"
shouted Boggle.
"I didn't know my beak came
with buttons," said Twit.
"Where is the buttonhole?"

Boggle and Bumf and Baffle
laughed and hooted. They
loved to play tricks on poor
Twit.

Chapter Two

"Time to go hunting," said
Baffle as the moon rose high.

"Oh! Yes!" Twit flapped about. "Where shall I hunt tonight?"

Bumf smiled. Here was a
chance for some fun!
"I hear there are lots of tasty
fish in the big round puddle."

Twit gasped. "I've never caught a fish before."

"That's because you are a twit," said Bumf.

"True," Twit said. "How can I catch one?"

Bumf smiled again. "Dive in and surprise them, of course!"

"Thanks, Bumf!" Twit cried.
"What a good idea!"

But of course it wasn't.

No fish lived in the puddle.
It was not deep enough.
Twit dived in and bumped
his head! "Ooow!" he
hooted. "Where are all the
fish? They must be hiding!"

Twit flapped and splashed in the water until he was cold and tired and shivery. Then he flew back to the nest with a rumbling tum.

Boggle and Baffle laughed
with Bumf. Tricking their
little brother was a hoot.

Chapter Three

The next night, Twit was very tired. That made catching bugs harder. Boggle watched Twit try to catch an ant that kept running away.

He smiled. "What you need, Twit, is a bug-buddy bear," said Boggle. "A bug-buddy bear loves helping other animals hunt for insects. She does all the hard work, and you eat all the bugs."

Twit blinked. "I've never heard of a bug-buddy bear."
"That's because you are a twit," said Boggle.
"True," Twit said. "Well, where can I find one?"

"There's a bug-buddy bear in the dark cold cave. Tell her to catch you some bugs and don't say please. Bears hate good manners."

"Thanks, Boggle!" Twit cried, as he flew away to find the bug-buddy bear. "What a good idea!"

But of course it wasn't.

There is no such thing as
a bug-buddy bear. A bear
did live in the dark cold
cave. But she was a cross and
mean bear.

Twit flew into her cave.
"You there!" he hooted.
"Go out and catch me some
bugs for supper.
Now!"

The big bear could not
believe that something so
small could be so cheeky.
With a terrible roar and a
swipe of her paw, she threw
herself at Twit.

"Help!" Twit flapped away as fast as he could, all the way back to his nest.

Bumf and Baffle cheered.
Tricking their little brother
was the best!

Chapter Four

Next day, Twit was still shaky. "Cheer up," said Baffle. "I know a place where bugs have parties."

He took Twit outside and pointed to a small hole in the ground. "There are hundreds of bugs having a party down there."

Twit blinked. "I've never heard of a bug party."

"That's because you are a twit," said Baffle.

"True," Twit said. "How do I get invited?"

"Push your head inside the hole," said Baffle, trying not to smile.

"Thanks, Baffle!" Twit cried, as he flapped off to the hole. "What a good idea!"

But of course it wasn't.

There were no bugs.
Twit got his head stuck in the
hole. He pulled and pulled
but he couldn't get out.

"Ha, ha, ha," laughed Boggle
and Bumf. "Twit is such
a twit!" And off they went,
back to their tree.

Poor Twit. Suddenly he heard something move in the dark.

"Hello," said a sleepy voice. "Twit ter-woo!" Twit twittered. "Who are you?" "I'm Norma, I'm a vole. Your head is stuck in my home."

"Sorry, Norma!" Twit wriggled
and jiggled, but it was no
use. "I'm Twit, by the way."
"Pleased to meet you," said
Norma. "Don't worry, Twit.
I can dig you out."

"What a good idea!" Twit
cried.

And of course it was.

Norma had Twit out in no time.

Thump!

Twit smiled at the little vole.

"Thank you, Norma."
"You're welcome." Norma
looked at Twit. "How did you
get stuck in my burrow?"

Twit blushed. "My brothers
keep playing tricks on me,
and I keep believing them.
I'm such a twit."

Norma smiled. "Everyone is a bit of a twit from time to time. But picking on people is a very twittish thing to do. You shouldn't let your brothers get away with it."

"But what can I do?" asked
Twit.
"Stick up for yourself!" said
Norma.

Then something strange
happened.
For the first time ever, Twit
had an idea of his own.

Twit whispered to Norma.
Norma smiled. "What a good
idea!"
And of course it was.

Chapter Five

Twit flapped outside and found the oldest, stickiest cobwebs. Then Norma helped him collect some squelchy mud from the stream.

The two new friends mixed
the mud and webs together
and stuck the sludgy mess to
a tree.

Then Twit flew up and sank
his bottom into the gloopy
goo.

It stuck him there like glue!

Norma gave Twit
a big thumbs up.
Twit smiled.

"Look at me!" Twit hooted, stretching out his wings. "Bumf! Boggle! Baffle – I'm floating!"

Twit's brothers gasped. It
looked as if Twit was floating
in the air!

Norma rushed about the
forest, waking up all the
animals. "Come and see the
floating owl! He's lighter
than air!"

Very soon, there was a large
crowd staring at Twit.

Little owls can't really float.
But Bumf and Boggle and
Baffle believed that Twit had
learned how to – and they
were very cross.
"Look at him!" cried Baffle.
Bumf stamped his foot.
"Come on, boys. If Twit the
twit can learn to float –
so can we!"

At once, the three big birds
flapped about.

But they could *not* float,
however hard they tried.

They flew this way and
that way

and upside-down

and bomp! into the tree

and pomp! onto the grass.

The more they couldn't float, the crosser they got, and the crosser they got the sillier they looked. All the animals began to laugh.

"It's not fair!" screeched
Boggle. "How can Twit float
when we can't? How?"
Norma grinned. "Perhaps
he's not as big a twit as you
say he is!"

Twit's brothers went on jumping and flapping and puffing and panting.

They didn't even notice when
Twit pulled his tail feathers
free of the cobweb-and-muddy
glue.
All the other animals gasped...
And then they started to clap!

"What a joke!"
said a stoat.

"What a trick!"
squealed a squirrel.

"Look at his silly
brothers, trying
to float for real,"
laughed the
bear. "What vain
little twits!"

"Yes, they are twits!" the other animals agreed. Still laughing, they went home – leaving Boggle, Bumf and Baffle red-faced and feeling very, very silly.

Twit turned to Norma.
"Thank you for telling me to stick myself up."
"I told you to *stick up for yourself*, Twit! But today, you've done both – and now every animal in the wood knows you're not such a twit after all."

Twit glowed with pride.
"Thank you for your help,
Norma. What shall we do
now?"
Norma smiled shyly. "Why
don't we catch lots and lots
of bugs for our supper?"

"That's a good idea," said Twit.
And it was.
It really was.

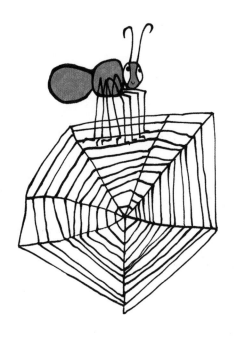

What are you going to read next?

More adventures with

Horrid Henry,

or go exploring with

Shumba,

and brave the Jungle

and Arctic

with Algy.

Find a frog prince with Tulsa

or even a big, yellow, whiskery

Lion in the Meadow!

Tuck into some

Blood and Guts and
Rats' Tail Pizza,

learn to dance with
Sophie,

travel back
in time with

Cudweed

and sail away in

Noah's Ark.

Enjoy all the Early Readers.